Peter Pan

J. M. Barrie

Level 3

Retold by Marie Crook

Series Editors: Annie Hughes and Melanie Williams

Pearson Education Limited
Edinburgh Gate, Harlow,
Essex CM20 2JE, England
and Associated Companies throughout the world.

ISBN 978-0-582-46140-6

This adaptation first published 2001 by Penguin Books

7 9 10 8 6

Design by Wendi Watson
Illustrations © Richard Gray 2001; p32 Bridget Dowy/Graham-Cameron Illustration

Printed in China
SWTC/06

Published by Pearson Education Limited in association with Penguin Books Ltd,
both companies being subsidiaries of Pearson Plc

For a complete list of the titles available in the Penguin Young Readers series
please write to your local Pearson Education office or to:
Penguin Readers Marketing Department, Pearson Education,
Edinburgh Gate, Harlow, Essex CM20 2JE

Once upon a time, in London,
there was a little girl, Wendy.
She loved reading stories to her
brothers, John and Michael.
Their favourite stories were
about Peter Pan.

3

Peter Pan lived in Neverland with his friends Tinkerbell and the Lost Boys.

'Let's go to Neverland!' said John.
'We can't go to Neverland,' explained Wendy, 'because we can't fly.'

But Peter Pan could fly. One night he flew to London with his friend Tinkerbell.

When they flew past an open window, they heard Wendy telling the story about Neverland.

They flew inside. 'Do you want to come to Neverland?' asked Peter Pan.

'Yes!' Wendy cried, 'but we can't fly.' 'It's easy!' said Peter Pan. 'Just think about lovely things!'

6

Michael thought about chocolate,
John thought about holidays and
Wendy thought about her mother.
It *was* easy!
They began to fly.

'Whee!' they all shouted.
'Let's go!' said Peter Pan.

7

Soon they were flying over
Neverland. It was beautiful.
'We are going to have a
brilliant time!' said Peter Pan.

But as soon as he spoke,
Wendy began to fall.

The Lost Boys were throwing stones at her.
'Be careful, Peter Pan!' they cried,
'It's a dangerous bird!'

Peter Pan laughed
at them and then
caught Wendy in
his arms.

'You *are* silly!' he smiled, 'these are our
new friends, Wendy, John and Michael.'
The Lost Boys *were* silly, but very friendly.
'Let's take them home!' they cried.

The Lost Boy's home was under a tree. There, Peter described his fights with Hook. 'Hook is a mean pirate,' he said. 'And he hates Peter Pan!' cried the Lost Boys.

'Years ago,' Peter explained, 'I cut off Hook's hand when we were fighting.'

'Yes,' said the Lost Boys, 'and now Hook has one hand and a hook!'

'I threw the hand to a hungry crocodile!' Peter said, 'and it liked the taste. Now it follows Hook everywhere, because it is hoping to eat more of him!'

13

When Wendy went to sleep
that night she was afraid.
But the next day, there were
rainbows in the sky.

'Let's go and play
with the mermaids
today!' said Peter.

When they were playing with the mermaids, they suddenly saw a ship.

They stopped their picnic and looked. 'Hook's here,' cried Peter, 'and who has he got?'

'Ahoy, Peter Pan!' said Hook, 'I've got your friend!'

Peter saw that it was his friend Tiger Lily.

'Help me Peter!' Peter flew quickly to the ship to help her.

16

The children thought lovely thoughts. Then they flew to help Tiger Lily too. They took her back to her family.

Peter Pan and Hook fought up and down the ship.

'You will never catch me!' cried Peter.
He pushed Hook and then flew away.
The crocodile was waiting to catch Hook.
'Aaagh!' cried Hook and he nearly fell
into the water.

Hook said to the pirates,
'We must find Peter Pan!'

They walked and walked until they
found the house under the tree.

Peter Pan and the others were there.

The pirates
listened.

'Neverland is too dangerous,' said Wendy,
'let's all go home. I want to see my mother.'
'We have never seen a mother before,'
said the Lost Boys.

They decided to go to Wendy's home. Peter said, 'I'm not coming. I don't want to grow up. If I stay in Neverland, I will always be a little boy!'

The children said goodbye to Peter Pan and started to walk home.

But the pirates caught them.

When they all shouted 'Help!' Peter Pan could not hear them.

Hook took the children to his ship.
He gave them pirate clothes.

'Now you're my pirates!'
he said, 'When Peter Pan
comes, we'll fight him
together!'
'Never!' they all cried.

Tinkerbell was with the mermaids when she saw the children with Hook.
'Hook's got the children!' she cried, 'I must tell Peter Pan.'

She flew as fast as she could.

24

Peter Pan went quickly to help the children. 'Hook!' he cried, 'Let's fight!' He climbed the ship's mast.

Hook followed him, higher and higher.

'To catch me,' said Peter Pan...

'...You've got to fly!'

But Hook could not fly because he did not have any lovely thoughts.
When Peter flew, Hook fell into the water where the crocodile was waiting.

'We must go home now, Peter,' said Wendy sadly. 'Remember me.'
'I'll never forget you!' said Peter.

This time, when they wanted to fly, the children thought about Peter Pan.

'Goodbye!' they cried
as they flew away.

Wendy's mother was very
happy when she saw them.
She agreed that the Lost
Boys could stay. They stayed
for many, many years.

The boys grew up and
they forgot Peter Pan.
But Wendy remembered
him.

When she had a daughter,
Jane, she described Peter
Pan to her.

Peter Pan never forgot
Wendy.

Many years later, Peter Pan
came to London again. He
was *still* a little boy!
When Jane saw him, she
smiled. Then she thought
about her mother, and flew...

ACTIVITIES

Before You Read

1 Look at the pictures in Peter Pan. Put a ✔ next to the things you can find in the book.

some mermaids	a castle	a book
a crocodile	a fairy	an ambulance
a forest	a picnic	a ship
some little boys	a pirate	some cats

2. Look at the picture of Neverland. Describe it.

After You Read

1. Colour the picture.
   Describe the picture.

2. Wendy, John and Michael think about lovely things when they want to fly. Think about a lovely thing. Write about it and draw a picture of it.